A rou...
Bad...

"Set... be the Top Dog of children's... magical debut of a book." Social Literary

"Kids' book takes world by storm." The Scottish Sun

"A moving and joyful story which warmed the heart of this cynical old journalist." That's Books

"First-time winner." The Evening Times

"A toast-loving, magical hound, who has been winning fans in book shops, libraries and schools across Scotland." The List

"A charming and very funny children's story." Diana Cooper

"McNicol & Jackson have created a charming new book character; a toast-crunching hound named Badger."
Aye Write, Glasgow's Book Festival

"A truly magical story which has all the hallmarks of a future children's classic!" Ursula James

"A magical 21st-century narrative which will delight and inspire folk of all ages."
Alex Lewczuk, Southside Broadcasting

"The toast-crunching, spell-muffing Badger the Mystical Mutt is a delightful, madcap, magical character, who worms his way into your affections." Maggie Woods, MotorBar

Badger
the
Mystical Mutt
and the Barking Boogie

Lunic★rn

...raising your spirit

ALSO BY MCNICOL AND JACKSON

Badger the Mystical Mutt

Badger
the
Mystical Mutt
and the Barking Boogie

McNicol & Jackson

THE LUNICORN PRESS

THE LUNICORN PRESS
Glasgow

Text © 2012 Lyn McNicol and Laura Cameron Jackson
Illustrations © 2012 Laura Cameron Jackson

First published 2012 by The Lunicorn Press

1

Printed by Martins the Printers, Berwick-upon-Tweed
Designed and typeset by Taras Young
Set in 14.25pt Gentium Book

British Library Cataloguing in Publication Data
A CIP catalogue record for this book is
available from the British Library

ISBN 978-0-9569640-1-4

www.badgerthemysticalmutt.com
www.facebook.com/badgermutt
www.twitter.com/badgermutt

For Donald McKinney

Chapter One

"Ewwwww!" winced Badger the Mystical Mutt, burying his nose in his neckerchief. "What a pong!"

It was a half past elevenses and all was not well in the lane ... or in Badger's tummy.

"Not long now till toast time," he said, patting his gurgling stomach. "Once I crack my famous smell-removing spell, we can have our morning snack, and all will be well again."

Most mornings, Badger's job was bird-poo patrol. He had to watch his Big Folk's clean washing on the clothes line, and be alert and ready to bark away the birds with their low-flying poos. But today, even the birds had decided to migrate early, to escape the vile stench of the lane. And now, before he could enjoy his higgledy-piggledy tower of toast, his Big Folk had given him a far bigger task — to get rid of the smell in the lane. An unexplained smell ... a mystery stink ... a stench of the very worst kind.

To make matters worse, his latest smell-removing spell didn't appear to be working very well.

He held his breath and tried again.

"Charcoal rocks and mouldy old socks,
Cardamom seeds and corn that pops,
Mix up together in a cardboard box,
Take this stink and make it stop!"

He stood back and waited ... and waited. His tummy rumbled, the charcoal crumbled, and still nothing happened. He sniffed the air around him nervously. Then his nose wrinkled in horror as he caught an even bigger whiff of the whiffiest kind.

"How can this be?" wondered Badger, scratching his head. "I followed the spell to the letter, but it's got worse not better."

Just then he heard a loud hammering noise in the lane. He trotted to the end of his garden and peered through the crack in the fence. There in front of him, on the fence opposite, was a freshly pinned poster.

The official-looking notice read:

ATTENTION!

OWING TO A PONG OF THE PONGIEST KIND, THE PONG POLICE WILL CLOSE THE LANE AT NOON TODAY FOR STINK ASSESSMENT AND REMOVAL. THE PONG POLICE WILL SPRAY THE AREA WITH ANTI-PONG POISON. NO ONE MUST ENTER THE LANE UNTIL FURTHER NOTICE.

"Goodness!" thought Badger. "I could have fixed this without the Pong Police getting involved. I'm almost there with my smell-removing spell."

Suddenly, he heard a hullabaloo in the distance. He looked down the lane and saw the gang, led by Dodgy Dave, thundering towards him in a cloud of dust.

"Uh-oh! Who are they after today?" he wondered.

As they hurtled past him, Badger turned to go back to his spell and heard a tiny voice shouting after the gang:

"Dodgy Dave! Dodgy Dave! Wait, please! I just want to speak to you."

"Leave us alone. You stink!" shouted Dodgy Dave.

"I'm getting the Pong Police on to you," warned Snif.

"If you get any nearer, I'll keel over," whimpered Lennie.

"Go away pooperscoopersmellysnooper!" yelled Pickle, running faster.

"I've just had my breakfast. I can't bear it!" yelled Pogo Paws, zooming ahead.

Badger watched as leaves swirled and bin lids rattled. Suddenly, the smallest dog he had ever seen went flying past him in a blur.

"Well, that makes a change. I've never seen that before; the gang on the run with someone chasing *them*!"

Badger's eyes watered as the rotten

air stung his nostrils. He shook his head, thinking, "If I can sort this spell before noon, I could save the lane from closure. And get my toast!"

He padded back to the spot where his ingredients lay. Sparkles of light twinkled around him as he repeated the spell.

"Charcoal rocks and mouldy old socks, Cardamom seeds and corn that pops ..."

His tummy rumbled loudly again. "Ah," he thought. "Maybe I need my higgledy-piggledy tower of toast before the spell will actually work."

Even through the smelly yuckiness, Badger's nose twitched as he picked up the familiar scent of a freshly made toastie somewhere very close. Then, he heard the plinkety plonk tune of the local bakery van.

"Right on time," he smiled, as he untied his famous red-spotted neckerchief and spoke to it seriously.

"'Chief, I have a job for you. *Float, float, float away. Find some toast to make my day."*

Badger sat back confidently and awaited

his snack. 'Chief always came back with the goods and had never let him down yet.

At the bottom of his garden, a pair of beautiful blue eyes peered brightly through the crack in the fence as Badger stretched out, licking his lips. The sun cast a shadow on his sundial showing a quarter to noon. Suddenly, his nose pinched, the smell was getting even more icky.

"Yuck! I hope 'Chief hurries back. I'll have to finish the spell before noon or the Pong Police will close the lane."

Right on cue, 'Chief drifted over the fence and hovered above Badger's nose.

"*Yummity yum yum yum, must get this toast into my tum, then my magic can be done!*" Badger drooled, feeling very pleased with himself. 'Chief wrapped itself back around his neck and knotted neatly.

As Badger munched into the delicious cheese toastie, the blue eyes at the bottom of the garden widened and watched in wonder. The tiny dog that had been chasing Dodgy Dave and his gang skipped through

the crack in the fence and marched up to Badger.

"Ahem!" she coughed slightly.

Badger stopped mid-munch and looked around him, unable to see where the noise had come from, but the air reeked worse than before. He thought no more of it and finished the last bite of his toastie. It was time to get back to work on his spell.

A loud *prffffft* sounded nearby. Badger looked around him again, but still couldn't see what had caused the noise. He shook his head and got back to work.

Shuffling the ingredients, he rubbed two small twigs together vigorously.

"Charcoal rocks and mouldy old socks,
Cardamom seeds and corn that pops,

Mix up together in a cardboard box,
Take this stink and make it stop!"

As the twigs sparked and the clock struck noon, he heard another cough, an even louder *prffffft*, a big bang ... and everything went black.

Chapter Two

Badger and the tiny dog looked at each other, blinking. They were covered in soot from head to toe.

"What just happened?" choked the little dog, shaking the soot from her fur.

"Oh! I'm not quite sure. Something exploded." Badger frowned, scratching his head. Then he noticed a wisp of smoke rise from the tiny dog's bottom.

"Why were the twigs sparking?" asked the little dog.

"I was perfecting my famous smell-

removing spell, only it didn't quite work,"
said Badger raising an eyebrow. "Because,
I suspect, some sort of windypops is
connected with the sparks."

He untied his dirty neckerchief and held
it over his nose.

"And now the smell is worse now than
before. Hang on ..." said Badger leaning
down to sniff the other dog. One sniff was
more than enough.

"It's you!" shouted Badger, stumbling
backwards away from the stink. "You're the
cause of the unexplained foulness! *That's*
why the gang was running away from you."

The ball of fur next to him shook her
bottom indignantly and waggled her tail.

"Indeed it is not!"

"Who are you anyway?" asked Badger
more gently "I've not seen you in the lane
before."

The small dog puffed out her chest and
proudly announced, "I'm Cheryl with a C,
that's me, not Sheryl with an S, because
Sheryl with an S goes 'Ssssshhhh', whilst

Cheryl with a C goes 'Ch' ... as in cha-cha-cha!"

"Are you a Chiuhuaha?" he asked

"I'm a sausage dog actually; a chipolata."

"I don't think you're a sausage dog, Cheryl, but you definitely put the *wah-wah* in Chihuahua."

"Whatever! I've got a bigger problem than the smell right now," exclaimed Cheryl. "They've closed the lane!"

"The Pong Police need to get to the *bottom* of the mystery smell. Except I think we both know why the lane smells," said Badger, raising his other eyebrow in the direction of Cheryl's tiny bottom.

"But now I've got nowhere to practise," sighed Cheryl.

"Practise what?" asked Badger, still dusting off the dirt from his coat.

"My dancing, of course! I want to enter the *Hotpaws Barking Boogie*. But now I've got nowhere to practise, and no dancing partner."

"You dance? Are you any good?" asked

Badger, somewhat amused.

"Good? Am I any good? I am the very best. My cha-cha is world famous," she replied, sashaying across the garden. "But the rules for the *Barking Boogie* say I cannot enter without a partner," she added sadly.

"You're certainly full of beans, Cheryl. But maybe that's exactly the problem!" Badger smiled.

"They talk of you everywhere, Badger. You are the Mystical Mutt, and you can fix things with your magic. Can you open the lane again so I can practise my groove? Maybe you can help me find a dancing partner?"

"Okay, I will do what I can to help, Cheryl. But why are you after the gang? It did make me chuckle, to see *them* being chased for a change."

"It's Dodgy Dave. I've seen him ..." she sighed.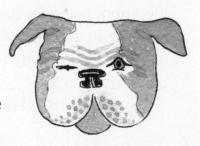

"Seen him what?"

"At night, under the

street spotlight, I've seen him dance a slow paw-shuffle. He's my Sugar Paws; my hero. He has put the jam in my jamalamadingdog." Cheryl clasped her paws to her tiny chest.

"Goodness! Dodgy Dave? A dancer? Isn't he a tearaway? Who knew he had some rhythm in his bones instead of four left paws?"

"He knows about the *Barking Boogie* too. Anton Du Bark will be the judge. But if the lane is closed, the *Barking Boogie* can't go ahead anyway and Dodgy Dave won't dance."

"How do you know he won't dance?" asked Badger

"Every time I try to speak to him, he runs away."

Cheryl looked up at him with her big, innocent eyes. Badger thought for a moment, careful not to hurt Cheryl's feelings anymore by telling her just how badly she stank.

"Maybe we need to get you smelling

better, and then Dodgy Dave will dance with you!"

"Do I really smell so bad, Badger? The gang keep telling me I stink." Cheryl's bottom vibrated with another long, loud *prffffft*. The smell clung to her.

Badger had to make Cheryl believe the truth about her smelliness, otherwise there was no hope for her dancing dreams with Dodgy Dave.

"Cheryl, I do believe that *you're* the reason for the lane's closure. So that's good news in a way, because if we can make you fragrant, the lane will open again and Dodgy Dave might dance with you."

Cheryl lowered her head and looked up at Badger sadly, her eyes brimming with tears.

"I don't know why I smell so bad, Badger. Can you do a spell to make the smell disappear?"

"Oh, Cheryl. I can do amazing magic. I can levitate toast. I can fly. I can even time travel. But I don't know about making your smell go away. I've been trying my smell-removing spell, but you saw for yourself … it doesn't seem to be working."

Cheryl dropped her shoulders and sighed. "Never mind, Badger. Thank you for trying. I'll see you another time,"

Cheryl clicked her heels, turned and tip-toed softly back to the bottom of the lane, her head hung low. Over her shoulder, she said:

"One day, you will see me dance, Badger, and you will be enchanted!"

"I know, wee one, I know," said Badger gently.

As Cheryl stepped through the crack in the fence, she found the lane deserted. The Pong Police had started their task, and were spraying the area, using big machines strapped to their backs.

Cheryl looked wearily up the lane and spotted Dodgy Dave hiding behind the bins. She sneaked up to him.

"What are you doing here, Cheryl?" whispered Dodgy Dave, "All of us are supposed to be out of here by now."

"So why are *you* still here?" she asked.

"I've got nowhere else to go. This is my home," replied Dodgy Dave.

"Where's the rest of the gang?"

"They have pals in other lanes who've taken them in"

"I've seen you dancing, Dodgy Dave," said Cheryl shyly.

"What?" he shouted aghast.

Just then four Big Folk's boots trundled towards them both.

"Uh-oh! Quick! Let's get inside this wheelie bin," yelled Dodgy Dave, pulling Cheryl with him.

The patrolling Pong Police stopped immediately at the wheelie bins and shouted for back-up. They loaded their deadly sprays and took aim.

Chapter Three

Cheryl and Dodgy Dave cowered inside the wheelie bin, listening to the commotion outside. Dodgy Dave peered through a tiny hole and saw more and more of the Pong Police gathering around them, with their back packs and their sprays. They were surrounded, with nowhere to run.

Dodgy Dave winced, both at the scene outside and the smell inside as yet another slow, low *prffffft* sneaked out of Cheryl's bottom. He turned to her in horror.

"What on earth do you eat to make you smell so badly, Cheryl?"

"Just my usual hot Mexican fajitas. Why? What's wrong with them?"

"But they're really spicy, Cheryl! Far too spicy for dogs. Right, how are we going to get out of this one? The Pong Police are loading their sprays, ready to fire."

"If only Badger the Mystical Mutt were here. He could help us with one of his special spells."

Dodgy Dave rolled his eyes. "Badger the Mystical Mutt? What could he do?"

Meanwhile, back in Badger's garden, his neckerchief started to unravel from his neck. It swirled around and pointed towards the lane.

"Whoa, 'Chief!" said Badger, "We're not supposed to go anywhere near the lane. Didn't you see the notice from the Pong Police?"

'Chief nodded, but beckoned Badger and pointed upwards.

"It's a flying mission then?"

Badger stood up lazily, straightened his legs and shook his bottom

28

until his tail whirred. Soon, he was hovering in the air above his garden. He followed 'Chief out into the lane and up towards the wheelie bins. There, he saw the Pong Police poised to start covering the bins with their toxic spray.

He heard a tiny cough and smelt an enormous pong, and knew straightaway that Cheryl was inside.

"Uh-oh!" he thought. "I need to create a diversion, and quickly." He looked up at 'Chief, who was still hovering in the sky alongside him, and whispered: *"Show Koo Ray, Show Koo Ray, create some wind, and make them go away."*

'Chief swirled and swirled until a mini

tornado swept down the lane. The Pong Police watched in confusion as leaves and dust spun and whirled around them. But it only made them more determined to fire their sprays.

"Well done, 'Chief, but it's not stopping them from firing. And if that poison is carried in the wind then we're all in danger. I'll try something else." He scratched his head, pointed his ears towards the crew's backpacks, and said quickly:

"Treacle, trickle, gunge and goo,
Change their sprays to something new!"

As Badger circled above, out of sight from the Pong Police, he watched them fire their sprays over the wheelie bins. But instead of a fine mist of poisonous spray, thick treacle covered the bins.

The Pong Police jumped back and ran away, baffled by what

was in their backpacks. Badger landed in the lane with a bump.

Dodgy Dave and Cheryl clambered out of the treacle-covered bin.

Dodgy Dave gave himself a shake, then fled. Cheryl shouted after him, and turned to Badger, a little bewildered.

"Come on, Cheryl. Back to mine!"

Back in his garden, Badger sat Cheryl down.

"Okay, I do think Dodgy Dave likes you, but I don't think your smelliness is the only reason he flees when he sees you. I think he's worried you'll tell the gang about his dancing."

"But why would his dancing be a problem?" asked Cheryl

"Because he's the gang leader, so he has to be tough. I think the rest of the gang might think he's a bit namby-pamby for dancing. He's a hard nut, Cheryl. He's been on the run from the Dog Catcher for as long as I've known him."

"But I have to have a dance partner for

the *Hotpaws Barking Boogie*, and Dodgy Dave is my best chance."

"Then talk to him about it. But don't do it in front of the gang. Now, let's see if we can work on my smell-removing spell, to help you in the meantime."

Badger tried and failed again to remove Cheryl's smell. She shrugged her shoulders and thanked him for trying.

As she slipped through the crack in the fence, she came nose to nose with Dodgy Dave.

Chapter Four

"Ah, Dodgy Dave, I've been looking for you," said Cheryl, looking up at him, and smiling prettily.

Dodgy Dave grunted and turned to go, but Cheryl jumped up onto his head and put her tiny paws over his eyes.

"No, stop! Don't run away from me again. I know you love to dance. I love to dance too. And it's the *Hotpaws Barking Boogie* this weekend. Please, Dodgy Dave, will you be my dancing partner?"

Dodgy Dave shook himself, hoping to dislodge Cheryl from the top of his head, but she clung on tightly.

"Please, Dodgy Dave?"

"I don't know what you're talking about. All I know is that I have an annoying smell on top of my head."

"But you love the merengue, the dig swivel, the jitterbug and jive." Cheryl did a few dainty steps of each dance as she spoke. "Your timing is amazing. I've seen you cha-cha, rumba, samba ... and you've got a sweet Lindy Hop. I've watched you in the moonlight."

Before he could reply, four menacing shapes emerged from behind the old oak tree.

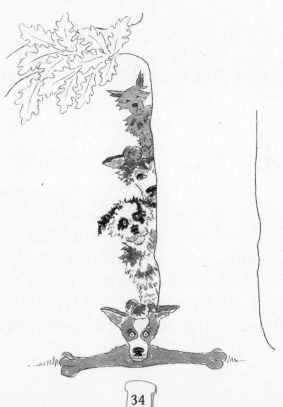

"Oi, Dodgy Dave!" teased Snif. "Why don't you show us your Paso Doble then?"

"Or maybe you could do a little pirouette for us, you wishy-washy dancer-doggie," scoffed Pogo Paws

"Did you put the *dum* in the dumdiddydoodoo?" shouted Pickle.

"No, he put the *diddy* in the dumdiddydoodoo!" sneered Snif.

"Oh, can you do the Slosh?" asked Lennie hopefully, kicking out his right paw.

Dodgy Dave grinned in embarrassment and said, "She's clearly mad, gang. You know she's always chasing us. She's bonkers. I mean dancing? Me? Never! That's for girlies, not tough guys like me."

Cheryl looked at Dave in disbelief.

"Badger said I should talk to you about dancing but now I wish I hadn't bothered," said Cheryl scowling, before adding haughtily, "You've got about as much charm as a squashed satsuma anyway."

"I might have known that Mystical Mutt was behind this. Wait until I get my paws on him!" shouted Dodgy Dave. "In fact, Pogo Paws, send a p-mail now to Badger. and tell him that our little pongy Cheryl here is unavoidably *stuck* in the lane."

Pogo Paws sped off to send the p-mail, while Dodgy Dave and the rest of the gang carried Cheryl to the wheelie bins where the gungy treacle lay, and plonked her right in the middle of the sticky mess.

Dodgy Dave smirked and said, "Right, Cheryl! Let's see you dance now!"

Cheryl used all her strength to try to lift her tiny paw out of the tacky black gunk, but with no luck.

"I can't move, Dodgy Dave. Please help me!"

The rest of the gang whooped and cackled as they watched Cheryl, who was stuck fast.

"Maybe Badger the Mystical Mutt will use one of his famous spells to help you!" sniggered Dodgy Dave.

Back in Badger's garden, amidst the general whiff of the lane, he caught the scent of a freshly delivered p-mail. He sniffed the lamp post to open it. It was clear that Cheryl needed his help.

He dashed into the lane to see Cheryl knee-deep in treacle, sobbing dramatically.

"Cheryl!" he shouted, "I'm coming to get you."

As he waded forward through the gluey mixture, the gang dropped a fishing net on his head and reeled him in.

"Gotcha!" shouted Dodgy Dave "Now let's see how you get out of this one, since you're so good at poking your nose into my business. Just so you know, Badger, the only dancing I've ever done is in a ring with Boxers.

"And as for you, Cheryl," he added, in his toughest voice, "you're not just *like* a bad smell, you *are* a bad smell, and you just won't go away. This should keep you in one place for a bit. Oh, and by the way, I'm sure I saw the Pong Police up ahead."

The gang snorted and chortled as they watched Badger slide through the treacle until he was next to Cheryl.

"You now have all day to chat about the delights of dancing together!" scoffed Dodgy Dave.

"Or until the Pong Police reach you," added Pickle nastily.

Dodgy Dave and the gang slithered off, leaving Badger and Cheryl in a sticky situation.

"Don't worry, Cheryl. I'll get us out of this. All I need is one of my most efficient sticky goo-removal spells," said Badger bravely.

Cheryl looked up at him hopefully and released another loud *prffffft*.

"Ooops!" she giggled. "I think nerves make my bottom burps bigger."

Badger frowned and tried his best to remember the magic words. Sparkles of light twinkled around him. "Bingo!" he thought, "Soapy suds! They should do the trick!" He tried to jump up and down with the excitement of remembering the spell, but his paws would not budge.

"Treacle, trickle, gunge and goo,

Time to turn into something new.
You're extremely sticky, and a little drippy,
So hubble some bubbles and now become
slippy."

If Badger could have moved, he would
have stood back with a flourish, as he was
very pleased with himself. Immediately, lots
of soapy bubbles started to appear around

them.

And soon, clouds upon clouds of bubbles filled every inch of the lane.

"Now's our chance to escape, Cheryl," said Badger. "'Chief, we need you to steer us out of here, please. *Show koo ray, show koo ray, out of the bubbles, up, up and away.*"

'Chief unwrapped itself from Badger's neck and billowed out like a parachute. Badger hung on with Cheryl hanging on to his tail. They climbed above the bubbles and soared along the lane, until they landed gently in Badger's garden.

"Well, that was a stroke of genius," said Badger smugly. Then, sniffing Cheryl, he added, "At least the bubbles have made you smell better. Not much ... but a little."

Cheryl brightened. "Oh, if the smell has gone, maybe Dodgy Dave will dance with me now?"

Badger looked at her kindly. "It's not that simple, Cheryl. I think we need to call in some extra help to get rid of your smell completely. Follow me."

Cheryl frowned and followed Badger to the sundial at the bottom of his garden.

Chapter Five

"This sundial," said Badger proudly, pointing to a stone pillar with a stone plate balanced on top, "is my Badgical Magical portal to the enchanted forest."

"What's a portal?" asked Cheryl

"It's like a door, which opens at exactly the right time for us to slip through into another place," answered Badger.

"I don't understand," said Cheryl, shaking her head vigorously.

"Okay, watch then. I'm just waiting for a cloud to pass and then we can be off." Badger was very still as he sniffed the air. He looked up at the cloud and hoped that the sun would peep out soon.

"Where are we going? I need time to practise my moves for the *Hotpaws Barking Boogie*," asked Cheryl.

"Well, this might help you find your dancing partner, Cheryl. So trust me just for a while, and I can assure you that you won't lose any time at all by coming with me now. Where *we* are going, time stands still."

Cheryl shimmied along Badger's back. She skipped onto the sundial and danced a cha-cha around its golden face. "What a great dance floor," she shouted gleefully.

"Ssssh, Cheryl. Show a bit of respect. Come back now," said Badger.

Cheryl hopped onto Badger's head and

hung on to his white tuft, wide-eyed at this magnificent structure.

"When the pointer on the sundial is lined up with that bone picture there," Badger pointed, "and that ball picture there, and when the sun casts its shadow in just the right way, the portal opens and we can take flight," stated Badger.

Cheryl gasped and said, "But it's nearly there."

"I know," said Badger. "Get ready, wee one."

As the shadow glided into place, a strange-looking contraption appeared before them, huffing and puffing, clanking and clunking.

"Meet the Wim-Wim for the Wowser to wind the weather up on a wet day," said Badger with pride. "Come on, Cheryl. Let's go and make you smell divine."

Cheryl hung on to Badger's ears as he stepped onto the first rung of the ladder. He twisted the big golden key that was sticking out from the Wim-Wim's side, clockwise.

As the contraption cranked
and creaked, jabbered
and droned, rattled and
groaned, they both took
their seats.

Sparkles of light twinkled
around Badger. The Wim-
Wim sighed and breathed out
a steady rumbling hum. Badger
nodded to Cheryl and shouted,
"Okay, we're off. Now I need you to repeat
after me:

"Open our hearts with our eyes closed tight."

"Open our hearts with our eyes closed
tight," repeated Cheryl, closing her eyes
tightly.

"Imagine our bodies filling with light."

"Imagine our bodies filling with light,"
repeated Cheryl, taking a deep breath.

"With good intentions clearly in sight."

"With good intentions clearly in sight,"
repeated Cheryl, starting to tingle all over.

"Let Badgical Magical Dreams take flight,"
said Badger with a salute! The top of the

Wim-Wim whirred rapidly.

"Let Badgical Magical Dreams take flight," repeated Cheryl with the same salute.

Just then a wondrous rumba beat pulsed throughout her body, all the way from the top of her tiny head, right down to the end of her tiny toes.

Chapter Six

"Woweeee!" shouted Cheryl, as she opened her eyes and looked around her.

"If I practised my high kick dance moves up here, they'd be the highest high kicks ever," she giggled.

She peered over the edge of the Wim-Wim and squealed in delight. "Everything looks so tiny. This is the biggest I've ever been!"

Badger smiled and told her to sit down.

"Now," he said, "I'm looking for a very particular cloud. He's called Nippy Nimbus and you will recognise him from his frown."

Just then, the Wim-Wim hurtled off to one side, as a blast of wind blew them off course.

"Where did that come from?" asked Badger, a bit baffled. "It wasn't at all windy when we took off."

Then the Wim-Wim plunged rapidly downwards.

They both gripped the sides in panic, as Cheryl's bottom parachuted above her. Badger looked up to catch Cheryl's legs and spotted Nippy Nimbus blowing hard, his big white cheeks all puffed out.

"Oi!" shouted Badger. "What are you doing? We're coming to see you."

"You're not coming anywhere near me with that smell. Goodbye!" Nippy Nimbus drew in another deep breath, ready to blow them out of the sky."

"Quick, Cheryl. Pull that lever next to you." Badger pointed to the middle handle.

As she did, a massive see-through circular wind deflector emerged from the rim of the Wim-Wim. shielding them from Nippy Nimbus and his bluster.

"And now for some of this," said Badger, stamping hard onto a pedal on the floor.

Vroooooooooooom! The Wim-Wim soared suddenly towards the grumpy cloud at turbo-charged speed.

They landed with a bump on the brow of Nippy Nimbus whose eyes started to water with the smell.

"Now look what you've made me do. You've made me rain. I'll get a row from the Drizzle Doctors because I was supposed be dry today," he complained. "Right, let's get this over with as quickly as possible. Usual place then is it, Badger? I need the password."

"Cloud number nine," yelled Badger confidently.

"Nope! You should know by now that the password changes with the weather," said Nippy smugly.

"Hmmph!" Badger sighed and scratched his head. He looked down hopefully at his neckerchief for inspiration. The Wim-Wim spluttered and the sun symbol hanging from its canopy began to glow brightly. Badger smiled and said:

"What about '*sunshine on a rainy day*', Nippy?"

Nippy groaned and said: "I don't know how you do it, Badger, but I'll catch you out one day. Okay, be on your way. At least it means the smell goes with you."

The important key on the side of the Wim-Wim started to vibrate and shine.

"Okay, Cheryl, here we go. Hold on tight," said Badger.

The Wim-Wim creaked and clattered, and panted and puttered, and in the cotton-wool fuzziness, an opening appeared. The Wim-Wim sped through it and, in the blink of a blink, they landed in a place unlike anywhere Cheryl had seen before.

"Well, this certainly isn't the lane!" she exclaimed, jumping down the ladder.

"Hang on!" said Badger. "Wait for me!" He rushed after her.

The trees overhead showered sparkles of raindrops on Cheryl's upturned face. She splashed gaily through the puddles. As she twirled her way through the flower stems, their petals sheltered her like a tent of umbrellas. The bees buzzed and the crickets whirred.

Cheryl tap-danced through the fallen leaves and squealed, "Badger, look at all the gorgeous colours. This place is amazing!"

Badger smiled at Cheryl's zest for beauty. "Come on. There's someone I want you to meet." She took his outstretched paw in hers and skipped along beside him.

They set off down the golden-leaved path. Soon, they saw a white wooden sign ahead.

"Ooooh, Badger, what's that?" asked Cheryl, dragging him towards it.

The sign had an arrow on it with the words: "*Boat Trips allowed. Fishing for Wishes permitted.*"

Cheryl did several star jumps, spun around and looked beseechingly at Badger.

"Please, can we go? Do we have time?" she begged, her eyes wide with hope.

"Okay, wee one. Remember, time stands still here, so we're in no rush. Let's go."

As they walked off the path, they saw another sign, which read:

"*WARNING! Be careful what you*

wish for; you just might get it."

"I know exactly what I'm wishing for, Badger. I want to dance with Dodgy Dave."

They carried on through the forest and soon heard the soothing sound of water lapping. Another sign, stuck into the mud at a jaunty angle, read:

"*Welcome to the Wishing Lake in the Sky. Please take a paper boat from the paper boat dispenser below and follow the instructions inside.*"

Cheryl looked up at Badger and asked, "May I?"

Badger nodded and let go of her paw. She skipped excitedly over to the dispenser, and took a paper boat. Inside, there was a folded

up piece of paper which Cheryl unfolded
quickly, reading its instructions aloud:

"Now you have your paper boat,
make your wish and make it float.
Think about your heart's desire,
the thing that sets your soul on fire,
your deepest and most cherished wish.
then set it sail with a precious kiss.
The Wishing Lake can make it true,
so trust in it, and it will you."

She looked round at Badger with longing
in her big blue eyes. Badger smiled and said:
"On you go, Cheryl. I'll wait over here." He
rested his bottom on the trunk of a big old
tree and watched her fondly. She took her

paper boat to the side of the lake, stood for a moment, and thought very hard. Then she whispered into the paper boat cupped in her paws, and set it softly onto the water with a kiss. Curtsying after it, she watched it sail across the lake, then climbed back up the bank towards Badger.

"All done. Ready to go now," she smiled.

She took Badger's paw in hers and they continued along the golden-leaved path.

Soon, they heard a rustle in the leaves ahead.

"Ssssh!" said Badger nodding to Cheryl, though she hadn't made a sound. "I think Baby Unicorn has come to greet us."

"Oh, can unicorns dance?" whispered Cheryl.

"Unicorns can do everything," said Badger with a wink.

Out of the trees, a beautiful white unicorn appeared.

"A unicorn!" shrieked Cheryl "At last, I'm finally meeting one." She curtsied and clicked her heels, then said proudly:

"I'm Cheryl with a C, that's me! Not Sheryl with an S, because Sheryl with an S goes 'Ssssshhhh', and Cheryl with a C goes 'Ch', as in cha-cha-cha."

Cheryl sashayed her hips and asked, "Can you dance, your royal unicorniness?"
Badger formally introduced Baby Unicorn to Cheryl, and he bowed to them both.

As Baby Unicorn got closer to Cheryl, his soft white nose shrivelled in horror at the stench. He looked at Badger curiously.

"I don't want to be rude, Badger, but that smell is unbearable."

"Ah!" said Badger. "That's why we're here. We need to make Cheryl fragrant so she can dance with Dodgy Dave in the *Hotpaws Barking Boogie*."

"Okay. But I warn you ... this could be the biggest assignment you've given me yet, Badger. Follow me."

Baby Unicorn turned and headed off in the direction of a brilliant white light glistening in the distance.

Cheryl took Badger's paw in hers again, and they followed.

Along the way, they passed another signpost saying, "*Nearly There*", and another saying "*There*".

"Ooooh, Badger, we must be getting closer to wherever *There* is. I've always heard my Big Folk say they're 'getting there', and now, here I finally am! If only they could see me now!"

"It's all about the journey, Cheryl. Sometimes, when we get to where we're going, we forget the fun we had travelling."

Cheryl looked puzzled.

Up ahead, Baby Unicorn stopped at the mouth of a cave set in clear quartz crystal. There was yet another sign outside saying:

"Thank you for coming Here to There, which is now, of course, 'Here'. We hope you enjoy your visit. Come back soon, and don't forget to tell all of your friends 'Here, There and Everywhere'."

As the crystals of the cave opening dazzled and shimmered, Cheryl gasped.

"A stage! Spotlights! This is my moment."

She waltzed ahead, completely fearless and enchanted. Badger ran after her.

"Hold on, Cheryl. Baby Unicorn must enter ahead of us."

Cheryl stopped and curtsied to Baby Unicorn, who was just behind her.

"I do apologise, your royal unicorniness. I just see lights and want to dance."

Baby Unicorn bowed and carried on into

the cave, with Cheryl and Badger close
behind.

As Cheryl weaved her way through the
crystal cave, its stalagmites and stalactites
glinted and glittered around her, and she
could not resist a little groove on the most
dazzling dance floor she had ever seen.

Her paws tapped
and her hips swayed
as Badger thumped
his tail on the cave
floor beside her. He
picked up some rocks
and shook them in
his paws to Cheryl's
beat. Baby Unicorn's
horn flashed as he
wriggled his rump to
the rhythm of her
rumba.

As she finished
with a stunning
fandango, Baby
Unicorn clicked

his hooves and swished his tail. Badger gave her a heartfelt round of up-paws and shouted "Bravo!"

Cheryl curtsied and beamed with pride.

"You see, I *have* to dance. The rhythm runs through my blood like the very breath I breathe."

"I understand your passion now, Cheryl with a C. You must follow me and I will do my very best to cure you of your smelliness," said Baby Unicorn, his flanks still twitching with the rhythm and the beat.

Chapter Seven

Baby Unicorn turned towards the back of the cave wall where the rock was flat and smooth.

A blast of light surged from his horn and lit up the cave wall. An image appeared.

"Ooooh, a movie screen!" Cheryl squealed in delight.

"Let's watch," said Badger.

In front of them, they saw a hazy scene of a pup playing and dancing with a much older dog, who looked a lot like Dodgy Dave.

"Come on, son," said the older dog. "You're nearly there.

Maybe one day you can win a rosette like this."

The older dog handed a shiny red rosette to the pup which had the words 'Greatest Dancer' printed on it.

"I want you to have this as a reminder of how good you are."

"Wow. Thanks, Grandpa. But do you really think I could ever be as good as you?"

"Just keep practising, son. Believe you can, and you will!"

The screen on the cave wall went blank, then burst back into action with a picture of Dodgy Dave dancing an intricate step pattern.

"It's Dodgy Dave!" gasped Cheryl. "I told you he could dance.

Oh, what's that he's holding?"

Baby Unicorn, Cheryl and Badger all watched in horror as Dodgy Dave ducked and stumbled, as he was pelted by a torrent of tomatoes. He fell to the ground in a heap, covered in slushy red pulp, scrambling round in a panic to find the tatty red rosette he had dropped. Just as he laid his paw on it, a voice snarled from the side:

"Let this be a lesson to you, Dodgy Dave. Dogs don't dance! And certainly not dogs like us."

"We're fighting dogs, not performing pets. If we ever catch you dancing again, there will be one almighty brouhaha," growled a voice from the other side.

"And as for this ..." snapped another voice. Cheryl gasped as the faded rosette was snatched from Dodgy Dave's grasp. "Tacky trash should be in the bin," the voice continued.

Dodgy Dave watched in misery as his attackers tossed his grandfather's precious keepsake into a nearby wheelie bin.

"Good luck with trying to find that!" the voice cackled.

Dodgy Dave walked off with his head hung low and his tail between his legs.

The screen went blank again.

Cheryl was speechless. Her big eyes brimmed with tears.

Badger looked at her kindly and said, "Now, I think we understand why Dodgy Dave has kept his talents hidden. He's a proud dog. Perhaps, Cheryl, you can help him find the confidence to dance again."

"But he runs away whenever he sees me," fretted Cheryl.

"Ah, yes, but that's also why we're here," said Badger. "I think Baby Unicorn may be able to help us out with that. Watch!"

Badger and Cheryl turned their gaze back towards the cave wall.

A new image sprang to life in front of them and Cheryl immediately recognised herself on the screen.

"Goodness, it's me. I've always wanted to be up there on the silver screen. Look!"

The film showed Cheryl standing by her dinner bowl surrounded by tins of *Super Tangy Chilli Beans*, packets of *Nicy Spicy Fajita Mix* and tubs of green *Wacky Moly*.

In the cave, Badger turned to Cheryl and frowned: "Erm, is *that* what you eat *every* day, for dinner?"

Cheryl nodded enthusiastically. "Yes. I love it. My Big Folks like sizzling spicy hot dishes and I eat what they have."

"Oh dear, Cheryl. Dogs should never eat spicy food. I think we've just discovered the reason for your stinkiness," said Badger.

They looked back at the screen, but it had already fizzled out.

"Is that all I can see of Cheryl with a C?" pouted Cheryl, fluttering her big long eyelashes.

"That is all we need to see," said Badger. "I think I've got an idea to get you eating a healthy dog food plan, and save you from the Pong Police."

"But I like my food!"

"Cheryl, do you want to dance?" asked Badger in exasperation. "Do you want Dodgy Dave to dance with you?"

"Of course, it's my dream."

"Then trust me. We need to call in some Badgical Magical help. Let's get to the Wim-Wim."

A rumbling hum shuddered through the cave.

"Our lift has arrived," said Badger turning to Baby Unicorn and bowing his thanks.

Badger and Cheryl ran to the mouth of the cave and jumped into the waiting Wim-Wim.

Once they had both uttered the magical rhyme, "*Open our hearts with our eyes closed tight ...*", they found themselves back in Badger's garden, next to the sundial, near the crack in the fence.

"Wow, what a swell journey, Badger! I really did trip the light fantastic there." Cheryl sighed. "I'm famished now, after all that excitement."

"Ahem! Cheryl?" said Badger ."Do you need to have the spicy stuff today?"

"Well, what else could I have?"

"Leave it with me," replied the Mystical Mutt, as sparkles of light twinkled around him.

"Thank you so much, Badger. I'll see you later." And, with that, Cheryl skipped through the crack in the fence and into the lane.

The Pong Police were nowhere to be seen and there were still traces of treacle on the ground.

Cheryl hummed a happy tune and danced along. Suddenly, she heard a rumpus ahead. It was Dodgy Dave and the gang rummaging in the bins. She ran to catch them up.

"Dodgy Dave, Dodgy Dave. Wait for me. I have something to tell you!"

The Gang looked up, startled, as Cheryl marched up to Dodgy Dave.

"I saw your rosette. It was so pretty. What a shame those horrible dogs took it away from you," said Cheryl innocently.

"What?" shouted Dodgy Dave angrily "How do you know about that?"

"Badger showed me," she said.

"What's this about rosettes Dodgy Dave?" snarled Snif, who emerged from behind the wheelie bins, followed by Pickle, Pogo Paws and Lennie.

Dodgy Dave looked sheepishly at his gang, and said, "I don't know what she's talking about. The smell must be making her delirious."

"But I saw it ... you with your grandfather.

He gave you his winning rosette," she blurted out, remembering too late Badger's warning to keep Dodgy Dave's secret.

"Shut up, Cheryl. Go away and leave me alone!" As he turned his back on her to face the gang, he snarled, "I think it's time I paid a visit to Badger the Mystical Mutt."

Dodgy Dave sped off in the direction of Badger's garden, and the gang sped off in any direction ... away from Cheryl. She was left all alone, worrying about what Dodgy Dave would do to her new friend Badger.

Chapter Eight

Dodgy Dave raced down the lane and barged through the crack in the fence of Badger's garden.

But Badger was nowhere to be seen.

Back in the lane, Badger was busy sending p-mails to all the local mutts, asking for help. He needed everyone to rally round and donate a tin of their own *Buddy Bites* dog food for Cheryl. So far, he'd had no response and was trying to figure out a spell for conjuring up some *Buddy Bites*. He walked heavily back to his garden and came nose to nose with Dodgy Dave.

"Oh, hello, Dodgy Dave. This is a surprise," said Badger. "Can I help you?"

"Help me? You've destroyed me, you snooping meddling mutt. Why on earth would I want *your* help? I'm here to pick a bone with you and your prattling ways."

Badger stepped back as Dodgy Dave lunged forward, baring his teeth.

He gulped when he saw his sharp fangs glisten.

"Did I mention that I used to box?" snarled Dodgy Dave.

"This could get nasty," thought Badger and quickly tapped his red-spotted neckerchief.

"Show Koo Ray, Show Koo Ray,
Over to you, 'Chief, please save me today."

The knot in the neckerchief unravelled, flew towards Dodgy Dave and swirled around his head.

Dodgy Dave looked upwards and crossed his eyes trying to focus on the speeding cloth.

'Chief tied itself swiftly around Dodgy Dave's eyes in a tight blindfold.

Dodgy Dave shook his head and

staggered, spinning full circle with his paws thrashing around him.

"Where are you? It's all gone black."

"You'll see things better if you calm down and listen to me," said Badger softly.

"I can't see anything at all," said Dodgy Dave in a panic.

"Do you promise to behave?" asked Badger.

"Do I have a choice?" asked Dodgy Dave sourly.

"We always have choices," said Badger wisely, then added, "but in this instance ... no, you don't."

"Okay then," agreed Dodgy Dave through gritted teeth.

"*Show Koo Ray, Show Koo Ray, come back, 'Chief, and light the way,*" said Badger

The red-spotted neckerchief loosened itself from Dodgy Dave's head and flew back to Badger's neck. Badger tapped it with his paw in thanks.

Dodgy Dave shook himself and widened his eyes in the brightness.

"I can see again."

"Good, but I'd like to help you see things more clearly, Dodgy Dave."

"What you are talking about?"

"The red rosette from your grandfather, and how you adore dancing!"

Dodgy Dave breathed out a long, slow sigh.

"How do you and Cheryl know about that? Thanks to you, the gang now know too, and I've kept that secret for so many years."

"You mean you've had to hide the thing you love the most. because you're afraid of what the others may think and do? Are you ashamed of having a dream?"

Dodgy Dave lowered his head and whispered, "I've never been able to talk to anyone other than my grandpa about it. He was a champion dancer. He encouraged me to dance. Then I got in with the Boxer dogs and followed them onto the streets."

"And they didn't think dancing was something fighting dogs like you should do?"

Dodgy Dave shook his head.

"So you had to obey them?"

Dodgy Dave nodded.

"Why?" asked Badger gently.

"Because I wanted to be like them, and be liked by them."

"I've seen you dance, Dodgy Dave. I've never seen anything like it. You have such a talent."

Dodgy Dave blushed.

"Do you think they were right to stop you from dancing?" continued Badger.

"Well, *they* didn't dance," answered Dodgy Dave.

"So, because they didn't dance, anyone who *did* dance was seen as different?"

"Yes," said Dodgy Dave, "different ... and a bit daft."

"Was your grandfather daft, too?"

Dodgy Dave bristled. "He wasn't daft, he was brilliant! He was the greatest dancer in the world."

"Then I think you know what you have

to do, to respect and continue his legacy. Why don't you partner Cheryl, and go and win that red rosette in the *Hotpaws Barking Boogie?*" suggested Badger kindly.

"But she stinks!"

"Leave that with me! I'm working on it," said Badger mysteriously.

Dodgy Dave brightened and bowed his thanks to Badger solemnly. Then he spun on his heels, did a sprightly sidekick and tap-danced his way to the crack in the fence.

Badger followed Dodgy Dave into the lane and sniffed the wooden fence. Bingo! He had received over 100 replies to his p-mail.

Operation *Buddy Bites* was underway.

Chapter Nine

Badger watched as a procession of dogs passed by the crack in the fence. They were all heading for one place — Cheryl's garden. In their paws they carried tins of *Buddy Bites*.

When Cheryl's Big Folk opened their back door, they were surprised to discover a pile of neatly stacked tins on the step.

Cheryl ran past their feet and stopped sharp.

"Oh my goodness," she thought. "*Buddy Bites!* They look tasty." She sniffed and sniffed, then sniffed some more. She looked up at her Big Folk, fluttered her long eyelashes and wagged her bottom.

Cheryl's Big Folk lifted a tin from the top and read its label aloud. "*Lickerish Luscious Morsels in Gravy Goo.*" They lifted another. "*Beefy Brutus Wellies.* Are these for you,

Cheryl?"

Cheryl jumped up and down and yapped hungrily. She followed her Big Folk inside, licking her lips.

"Packed with all the vitamins and minerals your dog needs to keep its heart healthy," continued her Big Folk. Cheryl thought about how her heart had been fluttering recently when she saw Dodgy

Dave. She hoped that *Buddy Bites* might stop the butterflies in her tummy too.

While Cheryl was tucking in to her new-found feast, Badger saw Dodgy Dave sidle past his garden. He walked into the lane and followed him. Dodgy Dave was also making his way towards Cheryl's back garden. When Dodgy Dave entered the garden, he looked around him shiftily.

Peering through a hole in the fence, Badger saw him add a tin of *Savoury Shoot Stew Buddy Bites* to the heap of tins on the step. After Dodgy Dave had looked over his shoulder a few more times, he pulled something out from under his arm and laid it down. Then he turned on his heels and ran back to the lane.

Badger hid behind the wheelie bin and, when he returned to his spyhole, he spotted a bunch of golden dandelions beside the tin. He smiled to himself and thought that Dodgy Dave was now definitely ready to be Cheryl's dancing partner.

A few days later, when the number of tins outside Cheryl's back door had shrunk significantly, Badger spotted the Pong Police in the lane, tearing down their old *Warning* notices and replacing them with a new poster. He waited for them to leave and ran up to read what was on it.

He read aloud:

THIS LANE IS NOW OFFICIALLY OPEN AGAIN, AND HAS BEEN CLEARED UNDER SECTION 111 OF THE PONG STATUTE, AS THE HIDEOUS SMELL HAS MYSTERIOUSLY DISAPPEARED.

"Well," he thought, "those *Buddy Bites* worked faster than I realised. If the lane is open, it means Cheryl is pong-free."

Just then Dodgy Dave ambled along the lane.

"I see the Pong Police have packed up and left," he shouted to Badger.

"Yes, it looks like things are back to normal again." He looked at Dodgy Dave, who seemed to have softened since he saw him last. "So now the *Hotpaws Barking Boogie* can go ahead tomorrow as planned. Will you be entering?" he ventured.

"I'd like to," sighed Dodgy Dave. "But I still need a dancing partner."

Right on cue, Cheryl skipped up the lane to join them.

Badger winked at Dodgy Dave and said, "I don't think you'll have to look far for your dancing partner."

Dodgy Dave turned to Cheryl and sniffed the air around her cautiously.

"Cheryl, you smell beautiful," he beamed.

"Thank you," she blushed. "The *Buddy Bites* are really agreeing with me. I loved your flowers, Dodgy Dave, and I liked the flavour you left best. You are very kind."

Dodgy Dave kicked his paws together bashfully, and asked, "Would you dance, if I asked you to dance?"

Cheryl curtsied and replied, "It would be my pleasure."

Dodgy Dave bowed, took her paw gently in his and they danced off down the lane together.

Badger returned to his garden and treated himself to a well-deserved higgledy-piggledy tower of toast.

"What a Badgical Magical job well done," he thought, feeling very pleased with himself.

Chapter Ten

The next morning, Badger was in the lane picking up his p-mails when he caught sight of Cheryl and Dodgy Dave up ahead, dancing together in silence.

"Have you two been practising since last night?"

They both nodded, then Dodgy Dave added, "But it's really tricky without any music."

"Ah!" said Badger. "I think I know who can help. Leave it with me."

He turned and trotted to the other end of the lane where the Alley Cats lived.

Trixie Rose, Velvet Viv and Silky Smith, the local moggies, were busy preening themselves on top of the wall.

"Hello, Badger," purred Velvet Viv. "Unusual to see you in *our* manor."

"That's because I have a favour to ask you. Do you still have your old Meowzik Maker?"

"We do indeed. Why so?" asked Silky Smith.

"Fantastic. Could you bring it to the top of the lane and make it play something groovy?"

"Of course. But what's in it for us if we do?" asked Trixie Rose.

Badger thought for a moment, then sparkles of light twinkled around his nose. His eyes brightened as an idea popped into his head.

"I'll teach you my special fishy dishy spell."

"That's good enough for me. Let's go, girls. We'll meet you there," said Velvet Viv.

"Wooftastic!" shouted Badger, already running back to tell Dodgy Dave and Cheryl the good news.

Before Badger could reach the other end of the lane, the Alley Cats had already arrived with their famous Meowzik Maker.

"What's that?" asked Cheryl.

The alley cats slinked around it and said, "Watch and learn."

When Badger caught up, he saw a large box with a big black disc spinning on top. A funnel-shaped contraption hovered above the box, and Silky Smith was sharpening her claws on a nearby stone.

The Alley Cats joined their paws together, then Silky Smith placed her sharpest claw onto the black disc.

Suddenly, Velvet Viv began to vibrate, until Trixie Rose shouted, "Stop!" She grabbed Badger and stood him next to her. "You're the woofer, now we need a tweeter!" She fixed her steely eyes on a nearby sparrow. The bird flew onto Badger's head and began to tweet. Trixie Rose pulled Badger's ear and ordered him to bark.

"Right!" she said." Hit it, girls."

Meowzik Maker

The Meowzik Maker burst into song with a *boom cha-cha, boom cha-cha, boom cha-cha* beat.

Cheryl's hips started to sway and her tiny paws tapped the rhythm.

"Come on, Dodgy Dave. We can dance," she shouted.

Dodgy Dave took Cheryl by the paw and puffed out his chest. They danced in perfect time. "Slow-slow, quick-quick-slow, dancing down the lane we go," giggled Cheryl.

They kept the Meowzik Maker running until well past noon. Dodgy Dave and Cheryl took a bow, and thanked Badger and the Alley Cats for all their hard work, not forgetting the sparrow for its tuneful tweets.

"I must go and rest now, to be ready for the finale tonight," panted Cheryl.

"If you shake those hips like that tonight, you'll get top marks," purred Trixie Rose.

Cheryl blushed. "Thank you so much, Trixie. I'm going to wear my lucky pink sequinned collar and my silver locket."

"Wow, Dodgy Dave, you rock!" said Badger appreciatively.

"Thanks, Badger. I'm still a bit nervous about the gang showing up," said Dodgy Dave.

"Remember your grandfather and you'll be just fine," said Badger, patting his back.

Later that night, all the animals were assembled in the concrete alley at the end of the lane, for the finale of the *Hotpaws Barking Boogie*. The bins had been polished, the litter had been moved and the ground had been swept. Badger stood at the back, watching and waiting. The gang fidgeted at the side.

Big Folk Anton Du Bark, the show's producer, sat behind the judging panel awaiting the first dancing dogs.

An Afghan hound and a whippet took the floor and danced an upbeat jive to a jumping rhythm.

"They just look stupid dancing like that," Snif sneered to the rest of the gang, who all nodded in agreement.

When they finished the judges held up their score cards: five paws, four paws and seven paws, totalling a good score of sixteen paws. Cheryl and Dodgy Dave waited behind the wheelie bins anxiously.

"The top score is thirty, Cheryl," Dodgy Dave reassured her. "So we still have a chance."

A white Scottish Terrier and a Dandie Dinmont were up next. They marched onto the dance floor, lifted their heads and danced a vigorous Highland fling to the sound of bagpipes and accordions. When they had finished they bowed their heads and looked hopefully over to the judges' panel. One by one, the judges held up their score cards: seven paws, eight paws and ten paws. The audience gasped.

"Wouldn't those two be better off chasing haggis?" growled Pickle to the rest of the gang. Badger frowned.

Cheryl looked at Dodgy Dave and said, "We'll never beat that. That was amazing. They got twenty-five out of thirty. That's almost a full round of up-paws."

"We can only do our best, Cheryl. Come on. We're next! Let's just enjoy ourselves."

As Dodgy Dave led Cheryl out onto the floor, the Alley Cats made an appearance and shook their shakers at the side. The gang looked at each other in utter horror. How could their leader, Dodgy Dave, embarrass them like this?

When the music started, Dodgy Dave moved towards Cheryl in a slow paw shuffle then Cheryl sashayed around him to the mambo beat. They looked like they had been dancing together all their lives. They were so swept up in their cha-cha-cha that Anton Du Bark had to tell them their time was up.

They stopped reluctantly, bowed and looked around at the audience who was in raptures. Nervously, they waited for the results. The judges talked amongst themselves and then Anton Du Bark was the first to hold up his score card. It was a TEN!

Cheryl took a sharp intake of breath, and Dodgy Dave squeezed her paw in excitement.

The next scorecard was held up. It, too, was a TEN.

The audience, Badger, Cheryl and Dodgy Dave all held their breath.

At last, the final scorecard was raised.

The crowd screamed and Cheryl fainted. Another TEN! In all the previous *Hotpaws*

Barking Boogies, no couple had ever received a full score of thirty.

Anton Du Bark tapped his microphone and announced, "As winners of this year's *Hotpaws Barking Boogie*, would Cheryl and Dodgy Dave please take the floor again?"

Dodgy Dave gently patted Cheryl's face and whispered, "Come on, Cheryl. This is our moment. We've won!"

Cheryl's eyes opened wide and she shook herself. Dodgy Dave held out his paw and helped her up. They stepped out onto the floor and Anton Du Bark placed a garland of flowers around Cheryl's neck. He then turned to Dodgy Dave and pinned a bright red rosette onto his collar. They took a bow and closed the show with a dreamy waltz.

Meanwhile, the gang were in an uproar, plotting Dodgy Dave's downfall.

Badger slipped backstage behind the wheelie bins to congratulate the winning couple.

"I owe you a huge thank you, Badger," said Dodgy Dave. "You gave me the courage to do this. I don't know how I can go back to the gang now. I just want to dance with Cheryl for the rest of my life."

"What's stopping you from doing exactly that?" enquired Badger.

"Everything," sighed Dodgy Dave. "I've got no home, no food, no Big Folk and my gang hate me."

"But you've got your red rosette, Dodgy Dave. You've got an amazing talent, and you've got Cheryl," replied Badger kindly.

Just then the gang barged past Badger and strutted up to Dodgy Dave.

"You," growled Snif, prodding Dodgy Dave's chest, "are no leader of ours. We can't have soppy softies who dance in our gang. We've had a meeting and you are dumped. I'm taking over as leader of the gang from now on. And as for this excuse for a dog," he added, nodding to Cheryl, "we'll make sure she never dances again."

"And you'd better scarper now because we've let the Dog Catcher know you're here," barked Pickle.

Snif lurched towards Dodgy Dave and ripped the red rosette from his collar. "And you won't be needing *this* either," he glowered, stamping the ribbon nastily into the ground.

Dodgy Dave looked sadly at the torn red rosette, and then at Cheryl. He held her face between his paws and whispered: "In order for you to be safe, I must leave you."

He kissed her on both cheeks as her heart shuddered, and her eyes glistened. Then he nodded to Badger, turned on his heels and fled the lane forever.

He didn't look back, certain he could hear the Big Folk boots of the dreaded Dog Catcher thundering after him.

Chapter Eleven

Cheryl stood, miserable, in the lane. She bent down and picked up the tattered red rosette from the ground and held it to her heart.

"What now, Badger? Do you have any special magic to bring him back?" she whimpered.

Just then, Anton Du Bark shouted to them both.

"Where's Dodgy Dave gone in such a hurry? I ran after him, but I couldn't catch him," he said breathlessly.

"Why? What's the matter?" asked Badger.

"I want to speak to our fabulous winners together. I've checked with Cheryl's Big Folk and got their permission. I have a marvellous proposal to put to both Cheryl and Dodgy Dave," he beamed.

Cheryl perked up and said, "Well, you can speak to me now and I can discuss with Dodgy Dave later."

"Well," said Anton, "the fact is that I want you both to be the stars of my new touring show. Cheryl, I want to work on your very own *chi-wah-wah* dance, and I've booked us in to Rio, Vegas and Blackpool for starters."

"Oh!" exclaimed Cheryl.

"And furthermore," he continued, "*Buddy Bites* are the sponsors of the *Hotpaws Barking Boogie*, and they want you and Dodgy Dave to be the faces of their new *Doggy Delights* poster campaign."

"Oh!" squealed Cheryl.

"That's the first time I've ever heard you lost for words, Cheryl," winked Badger.

"It's razzmatazz all the way. You'll never

look back, but you'll be on the road for a long time together. I take it you both get on?"

"But of course. Dodgy Dave is my hero."

"You better find him then and tell him the good news. We leave tomorrow, at dusk." Anton Du Bark turned on his heels and flounced off in a flurry.

Cheryl looked worriedly at Badger. "Tomorrow? At dusk? We have to find Dodgy Dave as soon as possible. This is a once-in-a-lifetime opportunity and we cannot miss it. I'll be sorry to leave my Big Folk, but if I can dance every day with Dodgy Dave, then my wish from the Wishing Lake in the Sky really will come true."

Badger smiled and said. "We'd better start looking for him then. Jump on my back, wee one."

In a street far from the lane, Dodgy Dave was weary from running for so long. He stopped by a street light and tapped his paws on the ground.

"No more cha-cha-chas for me," he sighed. "My only dancing will be solo from now on." He looked up at the yellow lamp and, out of the corner of his eye, spied a sign on a rickety garage door, which read:

"*Mighty Motors. Security Dog Required. Immediate Start. Apply Within.*"

Back in the lane, Badger and Cheryl scoured every nook and cranny: in the wheelie bins; in garden sheds; under grass cuttings; and the old worn out tyres. But Dodgy Dave was nowhere to be found.

Badger's tummy rumbled and he stopped to scratch his head.

"Why are you stopping, Badger? We have to search through the night. We *need* to find him," said Cheryl, getting more and more flustered.

"I think I need some toast," said Badger.

"What? Toast? How can you think of food at a time like this?" she screeched.

"Trust me, Cheryl. Follow me."

When Badger reached his garden, Cheryl hopped off his back angrily.

"You and your toast! We have no time for this now, Badger."

"Ssssssh," whispered Badger.

Sparkles of light twinkled around Badger as he closed his eyes and concentrated hard.

Suddenly, a large slice of slightly burnt toast floated in front of his nose. He caught it in his big paws and held it up close to his eyes.

Cheryl's eyes widened.

"Now, let me see," said Badger, peering at the slice of toast.

Slowly, an image appeared in the middle of the toast: a garage door with a sign saying *Mighty Motors*.

"Come on, Cheryl. I know where that is.

That's where Dodgy Dave
is. The toast never
lies."

Cheryl jumped
on Badger's back and
they set off up the lane
and beyond. When they
reached *Mighty Motors*, they
saw Dodgy Dave barking ferociously.

"There he is," shouted Cheryl in joy.

Dodgy Dave looked up from his barking,
and wagged his tail weakly at them. He
hauled himself to his paws and tried shakily
to stand, but fell on his side.

Badger and Cheryl looked in horror at the
chains and the iron cuff clamped around his
ankle.

"Don't move, Dodgy Dave," shouted
Badger, as he tapped his neckerchief and
uttered the words:

"Show Koo Ray, Show Koo Ray,
Find the key to take chains away."

Badger's neckerchief unfurled from his
neck and flew towards the garage door. It

slithered underneath and returned quickly with a ring of keys.

Cheryl and Badger rushed to Dodgy Dave and tried each key until they found the one that fitted.

"There," said Badger proudly. "You're free!"

Dodgy Dave tried to stand again, but with no luck.

"What is it, Dodgy Dave. Why can't you stand?" asked Cheryl anxiously.

"It's my back leg, Cheryl. I can't feel it at all."

Badger put his paw on Dodgy Dave's leg.

It was wet and sticky.

"I can't see in the dark, but it doesn't look too good. I think we need to get you back to the lane to have a proper look," said Badger.

"I can't go back there," said Dodgy Dave. "The Dog Catcher was chasing me when I left."

"That wasn't the Dog Catcher, Dodgy Dave," said Cheryl smiling. "That was Anton Du Bark, and he has a marvellous offer for us both. It's all going to be fine. You and I will be able to dance together forever."

Just then Dodgy Dave slumped. Cheryl flung her arms across his broad back in anguish.

"Come on, Cheryl. Can you help me lift him? We need to examine that leg in the light. Let's get him back to my garden."

Badger hoisted one of Dodgy Dave's arms around his shoulder, taking most of his weight, and Cheryl grabbed his other side. His legs dragged heavily along the ground.

When, finally, they arrived back in the garden, Badger lay Dodgy Dave gently down on the grass, where the street lamps from the lane shone their light on his injured leg.

"It's worse than we thought, Cheryl," said Badger grimacing.

Dodgy Dave had a huge gash on his leg. The iron cuff had cut it to the bone. Red patches of blood had crusted around the wound, but it was still bleeding.

"Oh no!" cried Cheryl. "He's never going to dance again."

Dodgy Dave closed his eyes and fell into a deep sleep.

A while later, he awoke with a groan. His leg hurt badly and his head was fuzzy. He opened his eyes to see Badger and Cheryl looking down at him with concern.

"Your leg has completely swollen up," said Cheryl. "It looks really sore."

Dodgy Dave caught sight of his injury and breathed out noisily. "That's worse than I realised. I don't think I'll be dancing again, Cheryl."

She turned anxiously to Badger and pleaded with all her heart. "Is there any magic you can do to help?"

"Let me think," said Badger softly. "Maybe 'Chief can help us."

He tapped his red-spotted neckerchief. It untied and floated flatly over Dodgy Dave's leg.

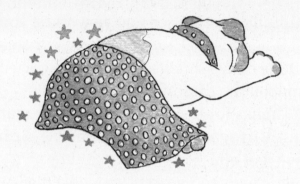

Badger knelt on the grass, placed his paw gently on Dodgy Dave, then uttered the magic words:

"Show Koo Ray, Show Koo Ray,
Use your healing magic to take the pain away."

Dodgy Dave was silent. Cheryl watched in awe as sparkles of light twinkled around the puffy leg. A few moments passed then

Badger stood up and said:

"Try and move your leg now, Dodgy Dave ... but easy does it."

Badger's neckerchief floated slowly away from Dodgy Dave's leg and wrapped itself back around Badger's neck.

"Thanks, 'Chief," said Badger, tapping it gratefully. "Let's hope you've worked your magic again."

Dodgy Dave flinched in pain as he tried to stand, but he couldn't.

"Thanks for trying to help, Badger, but I'm still in agony. My leg is no better. I can't move it at all."

Badger sighed heavily and looked at Cheryl sadly.

"I think we found our friend too late. The iron cuff has slashed his leg too deeply for even my trusty 'Chief to help."

Cheryl leaned over Dodgy Dave and patted his fur fondly.

"Never mind about the *Barking Boogie*, I just want you to get better."

Dodgy Dave tried to smile, then laid his

head on the grass.

"Perhaps a good night's sleep will help," said Badger hopefully. "Things always look brighter in the morning."

As Dodgy Dave's breathing became heavier and deeper, Cheryl and Badger laid down beside their friend, hoping that sunrise would bring good news.

But they were worrying more that it wouldn't.

Chapter Twelve

It was late afternoon. Cheryl nudged Badger awake, unable to believe that they had all slept for most of the day. She glanced at Dodgy Dave's leg, forlornly. Then looked again in shock. She gave Badger another shake as she looked at Dodgy Dave's leg in amazement. The swelling had completely gone and the red wounds had all knitted together.

Badger woke with a start. He had been dreaming of higgledy-piggledy towers of toast. As both dogs sniffed around Dodgy Dave's clean wound, he opened his eyes.

"Wow!" said Dodgy Dave, getting up. "Whatever your neckerchief did, Badger, it seems to have worked." He shook both his legs.

Badger touched 'Chief and quietly uttered

his thanks.

"Now I can't remember which one was sore," quipped Dodgy Dave.

"Right," said Cheryl firmly. "Now, no more security guard dog for you! We have a real job to do."

Dodgy Dave shook his head and said, "I don't understand."

"Don't you remember last night? We told you how Anton Du Bark wanted you and me to go on tour and trip the light fantastic together?" said Cheryl excitedly.

"What? I can't do that. How could I leave the lane?" said Dodgy Dave sadly.

"You left the lane yesterday, Dodgy Dave. We can now travel the world: Rio, Vegas and Blackpool."

"But I couldn't possibly leave my friends."

"Your friends?" said Cheryl impatiently "If, by your friends, you mean *the gang*, well *they* left *you*."

"But I won't know anyone."

"You know me, and Badger can visit us anytime, wherever we are, in his Wim-

Wim."

"In his Wim-What?"

"Never mind! I'll explain later. But now we must go, or we'll miss our chance," said Cheryl tapping her tiny paw.

"What are you afraid of Dodgy Dave?" asked Badger kindly.

"What if I'm not good enough?" answered Dodgy Dave.

Suddenly, Cheryl piped up, "Remember this?" and she held up his winning red rosette from the *Hotpaws Barking Boogie*.

Dodgy Dave's eyes brightened and he smiled.

"How did you get that? I thought the gang took it," he asked.

"I found it! Just like we found each other," squealed Cheryl, with outstretched paws.

"Do you really think we can make this work, Cheryl?"

"You better believe it, Dodgy Dave. Come on!"

And Cheryl and Dodgy Dave danced out

into the lane together.

Badger smiled, feeling in immediate need of some well-deserved toast.

As dusk fell, Anton Du Bark returned to the lane where Cheryl's Big Folk, Badger, the Alley Cats and even the sparrow were all assembled to wave them off. The gang, led now by Snif, skulked in the shadows.

"At least that's Dodgy Dave off our patch now," snarled Snif.

"Do you think we might see them on TV now that they're famous?" wondered Pogo Paws.

"Pooperscoopersmellysnooper! I don't want to see them ever again," barked Pickle.

"I'll quite miss Dodgy Dave," said Lennie

sadly.

"Oh get a grip, Lennie," snapped Snif, leading his gang away from the merriment.

As Cheryl and Dodgy Dave stepped on to the waiting tour bus, everyone cheered. The snazzy sequins on Cheryl's pink collar sparkled, and the red rosette, pinned proudly to Dodgy Dave's collar, shone.

As the bus trundled off, Badger headed for home, feeling very pleased with himself indeed.

Passing his garden fence, he spotted a poster for the *Buddy Bites Doggy Delights* tour with Cheryl and Dodgy Dave's picture in a huge heart shape.

Suddenly, his tummy rumbled.

"Time for toast," he smiled. "And about time, as this has been yet another Badgical Magical job well done!"

ALSO PUBLISHED BY THE LUNICORN PRESS

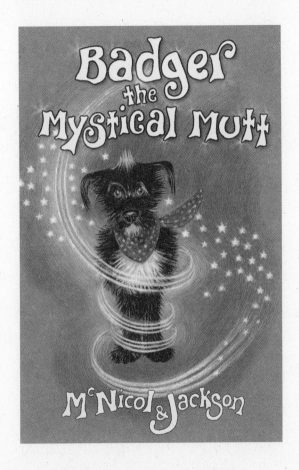

THE FIRST BOOK IN THE SERIES